Henry Bellyse Baildon

Rosamund. A Tragic Drama

Henry Bellyse Baildon

Rosamund. A Tragic Drama

Reprint of the original, first published in 1875.

1st Edition 2024 | ISBN: 978-3-38538-515-3

Verlag (Publisher): Outlook Verlag GmbH, Zeilweg 44, 60439 Frankfurt, Deutschland
Vertretungsberechtigt (Authorized to represent): E. Roepke, Zeilweg 44, 60439 Frankfurt, Deutschland
Druck (Print): Books on Demand GmbH, In de Tarpen 42, 22848 Norderstedt, Deutschland

Act IV. Scene I.

ROSAMOND ALONE.

ROSAMUND:

A TRAGIC DRAMA.

BY

HENRY BELLYSE BAILDON, B.A.,

AUTHOR OF 'FIRST FRUITS AND SHED LEAVES.'

WITH FRONTISPIECE BY H. H. NISBET.

LONDON:
LONGMANS, GREEN, & CO.
1875.

HISTORICAL ARGUMENT.

ALBOIN, the founder of the Lombard Empire, in the early part of his career of conquest, attacked and defeated the Gepidæ under Cunimund, whose brother Turimund had fallen some years before by the same hand. After his victory, Alboin conceived a passion for Rosamund, the daughter of Cunimund, and, upon the death of his first wife, Clotosvinda, daughter of Clovis, married her. In accordance with the savage custom of the race, Alboin had the skull of Cunimund whom he had killed with his own hand, converted into a drinking-cup, but this remained long unknown to his Gepidan wife.

At a banquet in Verona, in the presence of his queen, Alboin, having drank heavily, called for the wine-cup, and insisted on her drinking from it, not hesitating to reveal its history.

From that moment Rosamund plotted revenge. Helmich (described as " a confidential officer of the court ") was taken into her counsels in the matter, and his services secured by the promise of her hand, on Alboin's death. To Peredeo, a renowned chief and a formidable warrior, somewhat disaffected to Alboin, the project of assassination was broached, but he refused complicity. The queen was not thus to be baulked ; for, personating a mistress of Peredeo's, she went to his chamber, subsequently discovered herself, and threatened the chief with Alboin's vengeance. Perceiving the desperate resolution of Rosamund, Peredeo consented to participate in the proposed murder. One night, after the king had retired to his chamber, stupefied with wine, the palace guards were dismissed by the queen's orders; she fastened the sleeper's sword to its scabbard, and called in the conspirators, who speedily overcame the drowsy and disarmed monarch.

DRAMATIS PERSONÆ.

CUNIMUND, *King of the Gepidæ.*

EGMUND,
ALDOBERT, } *His Sons.*

ALBOIN, *King of the Lombards.*

CHEF,
PEREDEO, } *Lombard Chiefs.*

HELMICH, *an Officer of the Court.*

Captain, Soldiers, Minstrel, &c.

GODEBERTA, *Mother of Alboin.*

ROSAMUND, *Daughter of Cunimund, and afterwards Wife of Alboin.*

ALMA, *Foster-Sister and Maid to Rosamund.*

CONTENTS.

ACT I.

ACT III.

ACT IV.

ACT V.

NOTE.—The scene of the first and second Acts is laid in the territory of the Gepidæ, and between them there is an interval of some weeks. After the elapse of four or five years, the third Act opens, the scene of which, with that of the two remaining Acts, is laid at Verona. In other respects, the temporal arrangement is sufficiently indicated by the text.

ROSAMUND: A TRAGIC DRAMA.

ACT I.

SCENE I.—*Cunimund's Palace.*

CUNIMUND, ROSAMUND, ALDOBERT AND EGMUND.

Ros. O father, wilt thou yet again go forth
    To face, thyself, the perils of the fight ?
    Have not thy grey hairs won at length repose
    And respite from its dangers and its toils?
    O let thy people's and thy daughter's love
    Win thee to love thy safety, nor expose
    The king thy people prize more than their lives,
    The sire thy daughter loveth more than hers,
    To the fierce thrust of some exasperate foe.
    If thou dost fall, there is no victory ;
    If thou survivest, there is no defeat.
Cun. Nay, daughter, let no more such woman's words
    Dishonour her I thought had had a soul
    Lofty and noble with brave scorn of death,

Where death is honour, whom no coward fears
Found place in.   'Tis no loving office this,
No daughter's part, her father's heart to chill,
To shake his courage, make his valour dull
With womanish foreboding, and still less
At this, the hour when liberty and life
Of nations is at hazard on one throw,
On one fierce conflict, when the leader's heart
Must be a fount of courage unto all—
When once to falter is to be o'ercome.

Ros. Forgive me, father!   But I cannot bear
To think of Slaughter's swift, resistless flood
Breaking around thee, though thou, like a rock,
Dost bear thee up against it, and to me
My father, O the only nurturer
I ever knew, thou art too rich a stake
To set against a nation or a world!

Cun. Rosamund, would'st thou have me recreant,
False to my kingdom, falser to myself?
O Rosamund, thine is the only voice
That could unman me.   Would'st thou do it now,
When fear is ruin, hesitation death?
Yea, would I be the father thou dost love
If, at the very height of peril's pass,
I should turn dizzy and be faint with fear?
Nay, girl, this is unworthy child of mine.

Ros. O father, scorn me not.   'Tis fear of fear
That sickens me at heart.   Ye men that fight
And feel the heat of battle fire your brain,
Know not the chilling anguish of suspense.
Could I don armour and gird weapons on

How would I thirst for battle, how much scorn
A woman's fears ;—yet theirs the sorer task.
Yet go my father, and my spirit shall
Go ever with thee and, if love can bring
Fresh strength, fresh courage to thy arm and heart,
My soul shall be consumed in succouring thee.
Go, noble father, and my brothers dear,
Who, if he seem too old, do seem too young
For war's curst horrors ; yet I wrong you both,
For your great valour makes you chiefs mature,
His noble courage lends him ceaseless youth.
Yet be his body-guard : I shall not bear
To look on you again, if he doth fall.

Ald. Sister, the more we love thee that thy care
Is more solicitous for him than us.

Egm. Our bodies shall but be the shields for his.

Ros. embracing them. Farewell! Farewell! O may the
      God of battles
Shield you as surely as you shield your sire !
O father, father go, ere yet again
My fear can play me false. Almighty God,
Breathe dread and death before him ! Father, father,
I have no fear for thee, if thou dost fall
The bravest, best and noblest man there falls.

Cun. Now, Rosamund, once more thou art my child.
O God protect thee, darling, if I die. [*Embraces her.*
                    [*Exeunt* Cun. Ald. *and* Egm.

Ros. What ails thee, timid heart ? 'Tis not my wont
To quail at thoughts of battle or to tremble,
Even for those I love. Strange that to-day,
When desperate valour is our only hope,

I should turn coward ; but the phantom fear
That seems to haunt the trembling air to-day
And ever follow like a spirit-voice,
Forbodes misfortune, prophesies disaster,
Lays terror's icy finger on my heart
And mutters ever, 'they return no more.'
Away ye chilly terrors, Rosamund
To death and danger hath turned constant front,
Nor shall she flinch in this extremity !

                                        [*Exit.*

SCENE II.—The Lombard Encampment. Alboin's Tent.

ALBOIN *alone.*

'S death ! I can sleep no longer—I'm athirst
For slaughter and the noise of battle clangs
Through all my dreams and all the long night through
I hew down foemen who will ever rise,
As though I smote at ghosts and forms of air.
                                        [*Looks out.*
But now the stars grow fainter, as the light
Of dying eyes that flicker away to death.
                        Enter PEREDEO.
Thou'rt up betimes, Peredeo ; if thou hast
As hot a lust for battle as wakes me,
Thou hast not slept too peacefully.   I've slain
More in my dreams last night than e'er awake.

Per. My liege, to seek a favour have I come ;
 And the desire thereof has troubled me,
 As martial ardour irrepressible
 Disturbed your slumbers with its shadowy war.
 I cannot with an eloquent array
 Of subtle reasons, passionate appeals
 And flattering sentences surround your will
 And make it captive. I fly straight and strike
 Fair at my quarry. Sire, my boon is this,
 That I may lead the ambush that is planned
 To creep in silence through that long pine wood,
 Whence issuing we assail the foemen's rear.
Alb. Nay, nay, my brave Peredeo, I have fixed
 The order of the battle and each man
 Is to his place appointed, nor shall change.
Per. Yet sire, methinks 'tis but scant courtesy,
 Thus lightly to refuse an easy gift,
 One weighing not 'gainst long fidelity.
Alb. 'S death! *lightly* said'st thou ? War is no child's sport
 To be so *lightly* played at. Dost thou think
 That I make war in such haphazard fashion,
 As think it matter of indifference
 What chief should fire the van, which guard the rear
 And who the crawling ambush should conduct ?
 Chef rules the ambush and you lead the van.
Per. My liege, I think you do my caution wrong.
 When hath it failed that you misdoubt it so ?
Alb. Dream'st thou to move me with such tyro's talk ?
 Have I unfailing led you to success
 To be thus schooled by you, Peredeo ?
 Faith ! I as soon would think to set a boar

To harry eagles nests, as you to lead
An ambush,—-you, a mad impetuous fool,
A battering-ram of valour.   Am I plain?
Per. Pardon, my liege.   'Twas my excess of zeal
That made me seek the honour you deny me.
(*Aside*) Gad's mercy! I must yield or he will rage.

Enter CHEF.

Here comes my subtle rival, curse upon him!
I'd like a game with him at hew and hack.
Chef. My liege, I wait your orders, and my men
Are all equipped and ready to go forth.
You're up betimes my lord Peredeo.
I hope thy suit was granted of the king.
Per. My liege has granted my accustomed post.
I lead the van and hear you lie in ambush,
Till we have done the fighting, and then fall
Upon the booty and the routed foe.
Chef. I much rejoice you like your post as well
As it befits you.   I prefer a task
Where skill and judgment, not blind bravery,
And brainless valour, may perform their part.
Alb. Good sooth, Peredeo, thy appointment now
Appears in better savour than of late.
Per. I take it ill, my liege, if you refuse
The post I covet and petition for,
That you should flout me; but mayhap you'll strain
An honest loyalty, until it snaps.   [*Exit* PER.
Alb. He threatens, does he?   But I fear him not:
I know his ' honest loyalty ' too well.
He's not the courage that is dangerous
In private enemies.   In heat of battle

He rageth on like an infuriate bull ;
But when his blood is cool he hath not heart
To face an angry mouse—besides to plot
He hath as apt a turn, as hath a bear
To thread a rabbit's burrow.
Chef.   Right, my liege,
Yet press him not too far ; 'tis said, sometimes
A dove in straits will battle with a hawk :
His fear might goad him further than his hate.
Alb. Now gossip we no longer.   To your post !
And see that you discover not yourself
Till the right moment—then we have the prey
Fast in the toils.   But few shall sup to-night.

[*Exeunt.*

SCENE III.—*The Battle Field.*

CUNIMUND, ALDOBERT AND EGMUND.

Cun. to Egm. Why lad, what ails thee, that thou grow'st
       so pale ?
   O God, he totters and the red blood drips
   From where his left hand presses on his side.
Egm. O father, I am wounded, and I fear
   One of thy shields is pierced beyond repair.

My limbs grow feeble and the sweat runs chill
Upon my brow.   O help me, Aldobert!

[ALD. supports him.

Thanks brother—lay me down on my last bed.

[He lays him down.

Some menial villain struck me, as I caught
A sword thou saw'st not, father, flashing down
Upon thine uplift arm, unguarded then.
Happy I die obeying Rosamund.
Nay, brother 'tis no use, it will not staunch.
I feel the warm tide ebbing and the chill
Creep up me.

Cun.   O my boy, we three shall meet,
  I fear, this night; for now afar I see
  The foemen pouring fiercely on our rear.

Egm. Leave me then, father, for I shall not live
  To feel the enemy's heel.   'Tis growing dark!
  I'm but a stripling, sister,—did my best.   [*Dies.*

Cun. No time to mourn thee now, my boy, nor need.
  Come, Aldobert, the foeman's steel must join us
  To thy brief-sundered brother.   Down they swoop!

Enter some of the GEPIDÆ in flight.

Stay, stay, ye cowards!   Whither do ye flee?
No respite, no relief, no succour there,
No pity, peace or happiness or hope;
Chains, stripes, a darkened life, a wretched death,
The cruel mercies of the conqueror,
Await you there.   Turn, turn, you yet may seize
The only boon that still is left for you
In your fall'n fortunes, honourable death!

[*They rally.*

Methinks 'tis Alboin coming, with red surf
Of slaughter borne before him.   Meet return
Is this for bygone hospitality.
I saw the whelp had metal.   Troth ! he takes
My bravest but as brambles in his path.
Well parried, boy !   Well struck !   Quick ! quick !
    Great heavens
He's cloven him to the teeth as I would split
An apple.
(*To Alb.*)   Alboin !   Alboin !   You but sport.
Turn hither, would you find grim settlement
Of this our quarrel, and the vengeance due
From brother for a brother's death.

Enter ALBOIN, PEREDEO, *and* LOMBARD SOLDIERS *driving*
    GEPIDÆ *before them.*

Alb. Be not impatient, father Cunimund.
I met a flock of sheep on my way hither
Who stayed my coming, the unmannerly fools.
Despatch the youth, Peredeo.   King with king
'Tis meet should combat.

Per. to Ald.   Faith !   Sweet youth, so far
From your old dam 'tis perilous to stray.

Ald. Nay, Lombard, bear thyself more courteously ;
I came to meet my death, but not with words,
Not to be stabbed with shrewish utterances—
Mayhap thy tongue is sharper than thy sword.
                            [They fight.

Cun. to Alb. Have at thee, gory slaughterer, who com'st—
God curse thee for't—to waste my happy lands
With blood and fire.   The barbarous north no more
Will hold thy brutish hordes in her torn breast,

But casts them forth to flood these peaceful fields
With violence and nameless cruelties.   [*They fight.*
Alb. Spare thy breath, grey-beard, for thou can'st not move
   A heart that knows no pity or remorse,
   But revels in all fierce and bloody deeds.
Per. Gad ! boy, 'tis not thy first fight though thy last.
                              [*Wounds him.*
Ald. falling. O leave me not to linger—with kind sword,
   Let out my spirit.
Per. running his sword into him. There, thou hast thy
      wish.
Alb. wounding Cunimund. Thy fields will be the richer
      for thy blood.
Cun. falling. God make thy death as cruel as thy life.
   May no wife's anguished tears drop on thy bier,
   No childrens' grief hallow thy sepulchre.
Alb. There, dotard, lie and rave thy breath away.
         [*Exeunt* ALBOIN, PEREDEO, *and* LOMBARDS.
Cun. O evil fate, O unjust destiny,
   That makes such monsters rulers of the world !
   What have we done, that from our native home
   By these barbarians rude and merciless
   We should be riven—all resisting slain,
   And wives and offspring in base slavery
   For ever fettered ?   More accursed lot
   With its slow-moving, joyless wretchedness,
   Than death's intenser, briefer agony.
   O it were easy dying, if we left
   A land secure, sons whose sagacity
   And valour in their noontide 'gan eclipse
   Our waning faculties and failing strength :

But now 'tis bitter; for my sons, both slain,
Lie stiff and cold beside me : all my land
Is prey for ruthless lust, merciless power.
And yet one grief unutterably keen
My spirit wracks, and will not let me die,
So great its horror.   O my Rosamund !
O dear-loved name, my child round whose fair form
My heart's roots are entwined—I cannot die
For thinking of thee.   Would that thou wert dead !
I could send up a hymn of thanks to God—
I'd weep with joy, to see thee lying now,
With thy fond head here pillowed on my breast,
Thy dark locks wandering o'er it, thy white hand
Laid cold in mine, thy pure face marble still.

Strange visions through my darkened brain will float,
A face will ever mock me being hers,
Yet not the same—there is a cruel gleam
In her dark eyes—O God her white pure hands
No more are white ! Oh is that stain of blood ? [*Dies.*

Enter ALBOIN, CHEF, PEREDEO, *and* LOMBARDS.
Alb. Yes, Chef, 'twas rightly timed.   We must confess,
I think, Peredeo, we were at a check.
Cunimund and his sons raged through our ranks,
Like wolves amid a sheep flock.   Though I bore
Impetuously towards them, yet I could not
Break through to them—his folk so hampered me.
'Zounds ! here's the old wolf's body, where he stood
At bay, when I burst through to him at last.
I left him here, pouring his impotent,

Wild curses on me—a right sturdy foe
And, lest too soon his prowess we forget,
His hard old skull shall be my drinking cup.
Per. My liege, 'twere shame to mar his stalwart corse
And leave it headless.
Chef.   Would'st thou not take heed,
Lest any of his race, though all thy slaves,
Should think it scorn to their admirèd king
And rouse them to fanatical revenge ?
Alb. striking off Cunimund's head. Vainly your pity or
your prudence speak.
Come on, old grey-pate, you and I shall hold
Together many a revel—(*Places it on his sword's point.*)
                              [*Exeunt omnes.*

SCENE IV.—*Market-place of the Chief Town of the
Gepidæ.*

ROSAMUND, ALMA, *and other* CAPTIVES *guarded.*

Enter ALBOIN, CHEF, PEREDEO, HELMICH, &c.

Alm. There comes the king.   How truculent he looks,
How cruelly and contemptuously he glares
Around him, while his hand impatiently
Hovers about his sword-hilt, as though loath
To leave, even this unhappy crew, alive.
O Rosamund, I fear we shall be slain.

Dost see a stalwart warrior with fair locks
Beside the king ?   He looks more pitiful
And seems to knit his brows upon compunction
And sternly gaze around him, now and then,
For fear lest he be thought too lenient.
I think I'll pray to have him for a master.
Alb. Bah !   Murrain on your mercy !   Such as these
Do but encumber us with plethora
Of captives and unserviceable chattels.
'Twould make a merry massacre to slay them !
Per. Nay, sire, you are bloodthirsty overmuch.
For my part, I can never flesh my blade
In unresisting wretches such as these.
Chef. My liege, 'twere wiser that you let them live.
Your men will brook it ill they may not keep
These for their slaves ; and if apportioned well
Each man may for his prowess have reward.
Alb. seeing Ros. Well, as you will.   (*Aside.*) I think I
see a prize
I shall lay claim to.   (*Aloud.*)   Helmich, dost thou
mark
That dark-haired girl with tearless countenance
And eye unflinching ?   By her rich attire
And queenly pose she seems of royal birth.
Go, bring her hither !
Hel. going towards her. (*Aside.*) Faith my monarch has
Good eyes for beauty.   How right royally,
How beautifully defiant does she stand !
(*To Ros.*) Lady, the king of Lombards, Alboin, sends
Your servant to conduct you to his presence.
Ros. 'Tis not our wont be thus summoned, sir.

But I forget how changed since yesterday
Are our inconstant fortunes ; for at morn
I rose a queen, yes, queen in all but name ;
For so my father loved me that I knew
No law, save my own will, and recked no other.
Nor can I yet assure me whether this
Be madness-coined deception or the truth.

Alm. O Rosamund, speak not thus haughtily ;
For wholely in this monarch's power we lie,
Like helpless birds entangled in a net.

Ros. What can they fear who know no fear of death ?

Alm. But, Rosamund, I am afeared of death—
'Tis horrible to lie so white and cold
Nor feel the warm life tingle in one's limbs.

Ros. Lead on, my lord, and we will strive to school
Our tongue and countenance to servitude.

       [They move toward the king.

Hel. O ladies, mend your cheer.　It is not Hate's
Or Cruelty's harsh tongues that move the mind
Of Alboin, 'tis the softer voice of love.
My princess, when his glance alit on thee
The angel Pity, a white-robèd presence,
Entered his soul and scowling Anger fled.

Alb. aside. O how majestically does she move !
No goddess ever wore more regal grace !
How well that haughty head would bear a crown !

Per. aside. A face and form imperious indeed,
But moving awe and worship more than love.
More loveable is she, who follows her
With tearful eyes downcast, or timidly
Raised in such piteous supplication up,

No spirit that is forged of human stuff
Could, seeing Grief and Beauty so ill-matched,
Yet working such a charm, remain unmoved.

Alb. Approach, fair ladies, and, if any fear
Of wrong or violence lurk with you still,
I pray you banish it.   Ye are my wards
And whoso wrongs you is mine enemy.
(*To Ros.*) Pray lady, though methinks thy stately mien
Bewrays thy royal lineage, by what name
Art known?   And of what parents dost thou come?

Ros. Of such, my liege, that it is strange to me
To be so questioned, but I hardly know
Whether I wake or sleep.   If now I wake,
Then have I dream't a long delicious dream.
Would I could lay me in its arms again !
My father Cunimund was monarch here,
His word was law, his valour was our boast ;
For, though the frost of age had long 'gan sprinkle
His locks with silver, he was young at heart,
As fierce and dread in war as at his prime.
Noble he was in peace and well-beloved
Of all his people, and two sons he had,
Who, though they were not grown to the full bulk
And breadth of manhood, brave and terrible
In battle moved.   These but this morning were,
And now they are not.

Alb.   Lady, grieve not so
They died, as every warrior fain would die,
Girt with the piled slaughter they had made.

Ros. And dost thou think that this will comfort me?
I never feared dishonour would be theirs,

Death was the worst I feared, and death has come :
Yet are they happier than I.   Would God
This heart that beateth so tumultuously
Were still and cold as theirs are !   For the fate
That lies before us of the name of life
Is all unworthy.   Is it life to drag
Slavish existence 'neath the lash and threat
Of harsh and unrelenting conquerors?

  [*Looking around scornfully on her fellow-captives.*
The ox or ass may toil 'neath yoke and goad ;
Ye cannot make the royal lion do it.
But, Rosamund, thou hast a remedy
That none can baulk—with this unfailing friend
       [*Drawing a dagger.*
She can defy her captors to the teeth.

Alb. Hold !

Ros.   Hands off, thou sceptred ruffian, or I die !

Alb. aside. What splendid anger flashes from her eyes!
 (*Aloud*) Nay, Rosamund, there is a remedy
Far sweeter, for no slavery for you
Is waiting—rather rule and governance,
As is the due of one so nobly born.

Per. to Alm. Pluck up thy heart, my fair one, let not tears
 Make briny streams adown thy dainty cheeks,
 Where mirth's sweet dimple is but half-smoothed out.
 (*Taking her hand*) This small soft hand is hot with
  grief.

Alm.   O Sir,
 He looks so fierce, and Rosamund's so proud.

Ros. Dost think to snare me with your flatteries ?

Alb. No, lady, to no vile or humbling lot,

To which thy dauntless spirit death prefers,
Art thou appointed and a conqueror
Needs not to stoop to flattery to his thrall.
I, who am king, know well the imperious pulse
Of royal blood, that boundeth full and free
Or, by restraint dammed back, bursts the great heart.
Of royal birth, no badge of royalty
Shall be withheld thee, moving as a peer
To Clovis' daughter; though by War's mischance
Kingdomless,—save for hearts thy beauty wins.
(*Aside*) Would God that I could give thee nearer
    place!
What! frustrate, Alboin? What! shall my desire,
Like horse vain-rearing o'er a giddy leap,
Pawing for foothold in the empty air,
Crashing with lost shriek to his death below,
Thus fail beneath me, who am conqueror born?
Nay, 'tis a momentary gust perchance
Of passion and unworthy purpose calm!

Ros.. Such favours at a victor's hands are nought
    But gilded chains. I'd rather groom your horse
    Or grind your corn, than, like a polished trophy,
    Adorn your triumph. Make me an underling,
    Slave of your slaves, and yet no degradation
    Can you inflict upon my spirit, but
    Your courtesy degrades me.

Chef.   Nay, fair lady,
    You treat as equals, and for your bright presence
    He barters royal rank and dignity.

Ros. And, doing so, he mocks me; for the victor
    And vanquished are no equals.

Alb.   But I sue
    As vanquished unto victor—nay, by heaven
    I do not!   Lord Peredeo, escort
    These ladies to the halls of Cunimund.
    See they be treated with due courtesy
    And served with as much honour as before,
    Save such surveillance as may bar escape.
    (*To the soldiers*) For any insult, injury or annoy
    Against these ladies wrought, the doom is death.
Per. My liege, not even thy commands can give
    Deeper devotion to these ladies' weal
    Than doth already move me in their service.
                [*Exeunt* PEREDEO, ROSAMUND, &c.
Chef. aside. That fool Peredeo is love-bitten too.
                     [*Curtain falls.*

SCENE V.—The Palace of Cunimund.

ROSAMUND AND ALMA.

Ros. Alma, I envy you, for you can weep.
    I cannot; and for a moment doubt my grief,
    Thus dumb, though knowing its intensity
    Forbids expression, as a boy's top stands
    The steadiest at its utmost speed
    And rocks, but when it slackens.   'Tis the stound
    O' the blow that deadens pain, and so I feel
    As though my great calamities had not come,

And but impended, with full certainty
Of falling.

Alm.   I, who cannot choose but weep,
Sobbing myself to sleep, waking with tears,
Admire your fortitude, who, being more,
Seem less bereaved.

Ros.   O this unpitying sleep !—
Drugging the mind to short oblivion
Troublous and broken, haunted by grim phantoms
Of formless woe, that pass and beckon and point
Incessant, inarticulate, that our grief
May stab us fresh at waking ; so the cock-crow
Is signal of my father's death, the radiance
Of morning, joyous once, makes me an orphan,
Brotherless, homeless, captive, kingdomless.

Alm. How bright the past ! My heart is weary of grief
And cries impatient, 'when will joy return ?'

Ros. All hope of joy is dead in me, my cry
Is for oblivion, for all mirth will seem
A desecration henceforth :—our bright past
Is inaccessible and far removed.
As storm-enveloped travellers, whose way
Lies onward, where the tempest's thundrous roof
Bows earthward, looking back, where black, torn
       skirts
Of cloud are trailed, athwart dim, vaporous air,
See, yet beyond, clear peaks serenely poised
In azure and lit uplands emerald ;
So we behold the irrevocable past.

Alm. Yet have we cause for thanks, our conqueror
Being disposed to mercy, to bestowal

On you of all your natural dignities
And rank, by conquest forfeit.

Ros.   O this mercy !
'Tis crueller than sleep and gives fresh pang
To our humiliation.   I can bear
Our rude constraint, even as a forest-beast
May sleep behind his bars, the primal rage
Of capture spent—but lead him forth, tame show,
 ` Among the people—he will snap his chain
And rend them.   Nor could I about his court
Walk, captive daughter of a conquered king.

Alm. What would you then ?

Ros.   The undoing of our fate
Alone can right me.   I foresee some crime
Monstrous, by this unjust disaster gotten,
Slow swelling in the secret womb of fate
Towards the birth-pangs, shall be yet brought forth
In anguish.

Alm.   Be not hopeless, Rosamund !
'Tis impious to accuse the will of God

Ros. More impious to give evil this fair name,
And give heaven's sanction to the guilt of man.
Heaven's will or no ; I front the grimmest choice,
E'er woman fronted.   Death is on one hand,
A shadowy shape, with proffered cup and veil,
Alluring me in silence with mute gesture
Of mystic invitation ; on the other
Is Ignominy, a dark viperous dungeon,
Where slimy reptile things coil and uncoil
Unceasing, like one monster, so involved
Is form with form.

Alm.   O Rosamund, speak not so,
    It makes me shudder.   Would that you would bow
    More wisely unto that we cannot change!
Ros. There may be taint of madness in my brain,
    Seeing to me two personalities
    Alone exist absorbingly, my own
    And Alboin's; unto him I cannot yield,
    Nor can I 'scape his presence by retreat,
    Since darkness closes on the track of light
    And morn pursueth close the rear of night.
Alm. You talk too wildly, let us to the air
    O' the court awhile, seeing we have permission.
Ros. O would that change of place were change of thought!
                                    [*Exeunt.*

SCENE VI.—*The Palace.*

ALBOIN.

No momentary gust of passion this,
But like a storm, that, rising with the eve,
Goes ravening all night the forests through,
Bending in surges black the ranks of pine,
Casting its victims crashing to the ground,
Till all its ruinous desire is sated.
As when some fortress, with defiant frown,
Has baffled me and the strong fascination
Grows stronger with delay, before her pride

Stern, constant and impregnable, I grow
The more desireful, and all Italy
Would not corrupt me from my purpose.

Enter HELMICH.

Hel. My liege, prepare thyself for tidings evil,
   And bearing grief peculiar to thyself.
Alb. Speak on, and do not fear that I shall weep.
Hel. Nay, sire.   I fear not tears, but those strong souls
   Who scorn the use of tears, are more terrific
   In anguish than the weak.

                              You know too well
   Why your fair consort came not hither with you.
Alb. aside. Unholy hope, art thou fulfilled so soon!
Hel. Since thy departure, she has drooped the more ;
   Learned physicians and rare medicines
   Availed not ; with mysterious delay
   She faded and, alas, she is no more.
Alb. Dead ? Helmich !   Nay, it is a villainous lie !
Hel. kneeling. A subject plays not with a monarch's
   pain.
Alb. aside. Smooth dog, and has he read my secret thought?
   (*Aloud*) Go! go!   How know'st thou this ?
Hel.   •   A messenger,
   With fear and weariness all pale and stammering,
   Declared it and delivered us this letter—(*giving it*).
   A consternation utter on the chiefs
   Then fell, and none dared bear to thee the news.
Alb. reading the letter. True—true !   Cursed cowards !
   Thou hadst died for it
   But that I need such daring souls as thine!
   Go ! go !   [*Exit* HELMICH.

Dead ! dead, my Clotosvinda :—
Wild nature bright and warm as flame, gone out !
Expiring with the expiry of my love.
Is then my wish become omnipotent,
Working unspoken like the will of gods ?
Ye powers tremendous, irresponsible,
Are ye my servants ?   Am I one of you ?

                        [Curtain falls.

ACT II.

SCENE I.—The Palace.

ROSAMUND AND ALBOIN.

Alb. They stood upon my path, and so they fell ;
 As all must, standing there,—most worthy fate
 For brave men.   For, as every pool and stream
 In one great inundation are immerged,
 So 'tis the office and the destiny
 Of all who dare to rival or oppose me,
 Borne back, o'ercome, and swallowed in my flood,
 Its onward rolling waters to increase ;
 Yet would I gladly bid them live again,
 Yea, would relinquish every rood of conquest
 To acquire thy love.
Ros.   Alas ! how impotent
 The mightiest to retrieve an ill once done !
 Vain protestations !   Seeing thou art powerless
 To animate the merest worm thy heel
 Chances to crush in passing—how much less
 Hast thou the power to cause one human life
 Rebloom.
Alb.   Death is my ally and I may not
 Break faith with him.

Ros.   Say cannot, cannot, cannot.

Alb. aside. 'S death ! Can these, Death and Love, defy
  me thus ?

 (*Aloud*) No mortal may reverse the wheel of
  Fate ;

 And, like wine poured upon the ground, the past
 Is irrecoverable—e'en with gods
 Beyond recall. The future, like wet clay,
 Is plastic to my hands and shall be that
 I will it and I make it.

Ros.   But thy future
 Repairs me not my wrongs.

Alb.   Whate'er thou hadst,
 Dominion and possession, revenue
 And power, shall be restored thee twenty-fold.

Ros. Thou canst not render me my father back.

Alb. A maiden, when she weds, doth leave her kin
 And yet is happy, though perchance no more
 She may behold them ; in new love the old
 Enveloped is and lost, as the bright sun
 Doth banish every star.

Ros.   Where is the love
 To quench me my affections?

Alb.   Loving me,
 Whose power and greatness level to the banks
 Of thy desire shall flow, as river full
 Doth rock the lightest weed upon its brink
 And fill each deepest pool and dark recess ;
 Thou shalt forget the evil and the good
 Of thy past life and learn to bless the day
 Now dark with thy misfortunes.

Ros.   Infamous !
   I love thee not, nor ever can I love thee.
Alb. Then thou shall fear me (*seizing her hand*). Unto few
   I give
   The option—helpless as these fingers fine
   Lie in my grasp, liest thou within my power.
(*Kisses her hand passionately*) Say fairest, proudest, is it
   peace or war !
Ros. breaking from him. War !   [*Exit.*
Alb. Yes war, as when great conquering hosts encamp
   About a haughty city, wherewithin
   Are stately fanes and marble palaces,
   And treasures full and store of costly gems,
   Begirt with battlements impregnable.
   No violent assault or fierce attack
   Avails them—they await the silent aid
   Of famine, that shall open from within
   The ponderous gates whereon no blow hath rung,
   While yet no breach is in the battlements.
                           [*Exit.*

SCENE II.—*Garden of Palace.*

PEREDEO *walking about.*

'Tis just my fortune—one sweet waft of fagrance
Upwakens my desire and then the flower
By other hand is plucked—or, on a sudden,

Sheds all the petals of its beauty down,
Pathetically lovely in its ruin,
But scattered, soiled and irreplaceable,
Or, having swayed a moment to my reach,
Springs swiftly high beyond it. So, even now,
I have but held her little hand,—unconscious
In the distraction of her fear and grief
What passion throbbed in mine—

Alm. coming from behind a cypress. O prudent warrior!
You make a cypress-tree your confidant
And, even to her, you, sapiently, divulged not
The lady's name. Come, tell me.

Per.   What is *your* name?

Alm. One question by another you would answer:
First answer mine, and I will answer yours.

Per. My answer is ;—both answers are the same.

Alm. You put me off with compliment—my name, sir,
Is Alma.

Per.   Alma ; liquid, simple, sweet,
As thou art—

Alm.   Not so simple as you think me.

Per. I love what's simple—

Alm.   So you do profess—

Per. The gentle, low, monotonous complaints
Of wood-doves—loving in the quiet firs,
Or stream whose silvern dash is aye the same :
And eve is sweetest, when but one white star
Shines lonely in the west ; the full array
Of night delights me not, as that one star.
There! its first pulse of light broke through the
blue.

See! now it brightens in the hollow crescent
Of yon black pine-clad ridge. Come nearer! so.
                    [*He adjusts her so as to see it.*

Alm. O now I see it.
Per.   Lean your head back a little
    Upon my shoulder—you will see it better.
    There now, don't move!
                    [*She obeys, and he kisses her passionately.*
Alm. freeing herself. For shame! you take advantage
    Of my simplicity. Now I will go.
Per. O stay—we may not meet again. To-morrow
    At dawn I leave—by absolute command—
    Nought else would take me.
Alm.   O I am so glad,—
    You did not go before—now I can find
    That *one* star for myself.
Per.   But I lose mine.
Alm. O you will find another—
Per.   None so bright.
Alm. Good night, good night—I'll not come any
        nearer.
Per. You will forget me.
Alm.   I will try my best,
    But fear I cannot.   [*Exit.*
Per.   O what tripping music,
    Like dancing ripples of a sunny stream,
    Her speech is; yet not sweeter than the portals
    Wherefrom it comes. Her very presence lifts me
    Into a higher air, and my dull thoughts
    Take wing and gather radiance in her smile.
    Farewell, my dainty lipped! For thy sole sake,—

That so our paths again may interlace—
I'll drink success to Alboin's suit to-night.

[*Exit.*

SCENE III.—*Cunimund's Palace.*

Rosamund.

Ros. O how my way is all around beset
With grizly horrors!—For a moment poised
Between them, I, with breath fear-bated, pause
And shudder, ere I plunge, as one who halts
Wolf-hunted on a precipice's verge,
And, far beneath, the rocks shoot up huge fangs
From out the inaudible fury of the waves,
And, close behind, the horrible pant o' the wolves
And hungry snapping of their glistening teeth.
Would God I had a greater soul or less!
A greater one, that could face blank-eyed Death
With a meet scorn, and deem oblivion's shroud
Better than living, like a tiger chained
With fetters ever wearing to the bone.
Or less, that lacks the courage even to gaze
On that blood-freezing skeleton, and turns
Resignedly to any lot that bears
The name of life and stoops beneath the yoke,
That hardly galls the unresisting neck.

39

Enter ALMA.

O Alma, I am weary of this war
Of chafing passions. Tell me! What dost think?
Alm. Think, love? Why think you are most fortunate
To strike the fancy of this mighty king.
This chance has like a sudden sunshine burst
Through sorrow's clouds. I hardly can feel sad,
Thinking what undreamt honours will be yours,
Sitting on high the mate of such a king.
And, Rosamund, they will not make us part
You'll not forsake me, Rosamund, I know.
Ros. kissing her. No, dear, we never have been separate,
Nor ever shall be. Alma, let us die
Together now—it is the better way.
Alm. trembling. No, Rosamund, O no, I cannot die:
Why should we now, since you are chosen queen?
Ros. Dost thou not see how much I must abhor
This slayer of my kindred? Could I love
The man whose victory was my father's death?
Alm. O Rosamund you make my blood run cold
With horror. Talk not so—what would you do?
To kill yourself is wicked and horrible.
I could not do it; besides it is not brave,
Not like you, Rosamund, to take to flight
From evil fortune thus; and then, you know,
How grand to be a queen, perchance to rule
The ruler of the nation to your whim.
O Rosamund, I wonder that ambition
Fires you not to the task.
                          Then, if you die,
You leave me all defenceless, desolate.

He will take vengeance on me, if you foil
His purpose and—Oh dear I cannot die !   [*Sobs.*
                    Enter HELMICH.
Hel. Ladies, I bear a greeting from the king
To both, yet chiefly to fair Rosamund,
The queen-elect, if so her mind incline :
For his most ardent love can brook no more
Doubt or delay—your answer he would have—
                    [*Ros. makes as though she would speak.*
Yet lady, not in haste decide this issue
Momentous ; for a monarch's happiness
And lives of many on your choice depend.
Hard, princess, were the heart that could not feel
For your forlorn condition and sad fate,
Nor know how cruel must the conflict be
In your torn heart.   Yet pause, before you cast
A life aglow with the fresh fire of youth,
A beauty newly bursting from its bud
To the full glory and fragrance of its prime,
A throne whereon like twin-gods ye may sit,
The boundless love and passion of a man
No beauty so completely captive led,
And last, the lives of many you might save,
Disdainful from you.   It is difficult
To turn our passion's tide so suddenly
From Hate to Love ; yet is it possible.
Blindly we hate our nation's enemies,
Unwitting ought of individual good
Or evil in them. You, a Gepidan,
Hate Lombard Alboin. He no doubt did hate
The princess of the Gepidæ, but now

Loves lovely Rosamund—would make her queen,
Doth worship his late enemy and sue
For mercy from his captive. So may you,
The queen of Lombards, love their king, Alboin.
Ros. That was a hope that flashed across my brain,
But momentary, ineffectual.
Hel. sinking his voice and approaching Ros. But though
        love come not, is it nought to be
A queen of such a kingdom, yea the envy
Of all thy sex throughout the land, the mark,
Whereto all highest praise of beauty's aimed,
The ideal after which each damsel fair
Is trained and trimmed? Better than lying cold,
Rotting corruption in the wormy mould.
Alm. O Rosamund, I cannot bear to think
That you should die. O give him answer fair.
Ros. I am o'erwrought—I yield—go say to him
Yes—I will be your queen.
Hel. kneeling.   My queen, with joy
That words but faintly shadow forth I hail
Such sweet decision—hail the victory
Of judgment sound, over the yearnings, true
But over-sensitive, of pure affection.
                                        [*Exit* HELMICH.
Ros. Hast ever in some horrible vision, when
The agony became too great to bear,
Cried 'would this were a dream' and straight awoke?
So, now, I cry, yet will the dream not burst.
But Alma dear, now go—thy life is safe,
And if it prove not sweet, then blame not me.
                                        [*Exit* ALMA.

My choice is made, yet hardly was my choice.
How subtle-tongued a serpent Helmich is!
Now must I steel myself to play my part,
Must cast away the pure and holy past,
Must henceforth seem the thing that I am not,
The loving, faithful wife and loyal queen,
Lend Hate the face of Love, and give Dislike
The mask of amorous Dalliance, and Despair
Clothe with the lustre of a feignèd Hope.
Upon Ambition's altar I lay down
All love, affection and sincerity ;
False to myself, I nevermore can be
Faithful to any other. Turn, O God,
Thy face away, and let hell laugh to see
The lep'rous change ! For this weak fear of death
For ever hath undone me, and I know it.
Yet shall I grasp my miserable guerdon :
Yes, yes, my choice is good—I'd rather be
A damnèd queen than a base churl redeemed !

[*Exit.*

ACT III.

SCENE I.—Room in Palace at Verona.

ALMA *and* PEREDEO *meeting.*

Per. Well met, fair one !   [*Takes her hand.*
                    Nay, I'll not release it.
This pretty captive has been here before.
Do you forget when first this swarthy palm
Was gaol to these fair fingers ?
Alm.   No, my lord.
Per. Then were these eyes, dark as the violet,
    Swimming with timid tears, and that white breast,
    Now gleaming through your garment, like the moon
    Mist vainly covers, shuddered with quick sobs ;
    Those rich brown locks, so daintily arranged,
    Strayed in the wild abandonment of fear,—
    This little nestling hand was hot with grief.
Alm. Yes, I remember, I was so afraid,
    And all your faces were so stern and cruel.
Per. All, Alma ?
Alm.   All but one, a warrior tall,
    With flaxen hair, blue eyes and fiery beard.
Per. You minx ! And did he come and take your hand ?
Alm. Perhaps he did ; perhaps, Peredeo,
    He has it now.   [*He kisses her.*

(*Struggling faintly*) She did not give him leave
For such advances.

Per.　　　　　　Stolen sweets, my love,
Are ever sweetest. But those are not tears
That make the natural brightness of those eyes
More liquid than before?

Alm. with a sigh.　　　　　I am unhappy.

Per. Why Alma, are you angry?

Alm.　　　　　　　　Not with you;
But my life is not happy here. I am
So lonely, for they love not Rosamund:
And so all shun me. Even Rosamund,
My playmate, though my mistress once, is cold
And loveless to me now. I cannot bear
To live unloved and loveless—as a child
I worshipped Rosamund, and she loved me
In her proud fashion; but she's turned to stone.
· Then, Alboin makes me tremble when I hear
　　him
Go clanging ponderously through the hall.
All look askance at me, as though I were
Accomplice in some dark conspiracy.
There's no one loves me, none that I can love
But you, Peredeo.　　　[*Falls weeping in his arms.*

Per.　　　　　　Darling, do not weep.
Peredeo loves thee so that all the kingdom
Besides united could not love thee more:
So, if a warrior's heart can quit thy pain,
Thou shalt be ever happy.
　　　　　　　　　　Lie thou here,
Until thy fluttering heart forgets its tumult

And learns calm rythm of mine.   Weep not! weep
   not !
There dropped a tremulous brilliant on my hand.
O rain-dashed rose, look up that I may light
Thy face to laughter !   Dost thou still remember
The eve we parted, how one star hung low
O'er the dark hills ?

Alm.   Too well do I remember,
Though I have striven to forget it, still,
Like some rare perfume losing not its power
With lapse of time, this memory does pervade
With sweetness the dark chambers of the past.
Yet feared I you had found another star.

Per. Nay, nay.   (*Aside.*) May heaven forgive me that I
   lie
Thus soothingly.   (*Aloud.*) Though, like the star,
   remote
Thou wert more dear to me than the poor candles
Of present beauties were, for thy pure ray
Made their dull flames burn grossly in my sight.

Alm. laying her finger on his lips. Let no more flatteries
   out, you naughty lips—
While I do murmur forth to him th' arrears
Of my amassed affection, telling him
How he rode hero in my very dreams
By night or day.   It is too long a task—
I will but look my love into his eyes,
That flash their silent answer back to me,
Thus cradled in a swoôn of full delight.

                          [*Curtain falls.*

SCENE II.—Room in Palace at Verona.

Enter GODEBERTA *and* ALBOIN *in converse.*

Gode. Alboin, my heart hath never been at rest
  Since first you made this Gepidan lioness
  Your queen ; for, though her skin be sleek and soft,
  Sharp are the claws the tawny velvet hides.
  There's steelly cruelty in those bright eyes.
Alb. Tush ! mother ! why dost play the raven thus ?
  But 'tis your sex's way, you're always jealous—
  Some other woman always loves or hates
  Too much or little for your taste, and then
  Murders, assassinations, poisons, plots
  Embroil your brain, and idle, innocent hands
  Are mingling potions, clutching dagger-hilts,
  And guiltless lips whisper conspiracies.
Gode. That is because we are more clear of sight,
    Can pierce beneath feigned smiles and treacherous
      gloss
    Of pretty speeches and deceitful sighs—
    Can catch the stealthy flash of hate, where love
    Is simulated.   Who should know our wiles
    So well as we ?   For many of us must
    Be where we would not, share a couch unloved.
    So, seeing no escape, we wear a mask
    Until it fits us like our natural face,
    And only we, if we, know it is there.
Alb. 'S life ! will you preach for ever on the faults

Of your own sex? They've faults in plenty, quite
Apparent to the eye, without the aid
Of your clear-eyed witchcraft to see them with.
Gode. How can you dream of faithfulness in one
Who was your thrall, who had no choice but wed
The conqueror-of her nation, the destroyer
Of all her kindred? Do you see in her
The clinging and dependent tenderness
With which fond wives upon their husbands lean?
She moves so proudly, so aloof from all,
So isolate and coldly self-contained.
Alb. Will you revile her to the crack of doom?
She is my queen and worthy of the place.
Is she a lioness? The better mate,
Then, for a lion. Would you have my queen
Toy all day with me like a courtezan,
Or cringe before me like a frightened child,
Or would you have her sitting cheek by jowl
With maids and lackeys? 'Zounds! I made good
    choice.
Hast seen a statelier mien, more regal gait,
More queenly carriage or more lovely scorn?
What other woman hast thou feigned or seen
More fitly fashioned to become my queen?
The truest hound will answer to no call
Except his master's. Rosamund is cold
To all save me. The truer, then, to me.
I plucked her from the maw of such a fate,
So loathsome to her, she had rather shed
Her blood herself than brook its ignominy.
Is it for this she'd murder me forsooth?

'S blood, dame! were any tongue but yours to wag
So poisonously against her, 'twould full soon
Want place to wag in. You may croak you hoarse ;
I never sought your counsel on't, nor ask
Now for your warning. Here comes Rosamund.
Ha! you don't care to face her. [*Exit* GODEBERTA.
    Enter ROSAMUND.

                Well, my queen?
Ros. What, my lord? Parted angry from your mother
Or do I come unwelcome? I were sad
To see domestic quarrels weigh upon
A heart by kingly projects occupied.
I fear lest I should mar much happiness,
That else were yours, my liege. I fear you rue
That ever from that cowering band of captives
You raised me to your side.
Alb.   No, Rosamund,
I do not rue it, for my choice was good.
Ros. I would that I could move your mother's love.
I know my way is haughty. I can't whine
Submissively to any—she mistrusts
My cold reserve. I cannot feign a warmth
I feel not.
Alb.   Tush, girl! reck thou not
A rush for any. Thou are Alboin's queen—
Whoso wrongs thee is Alboin's enemy,
Whoe'er it be, and such have but short lives.
Ros. I would not stir your wrath, so terrible
And strong, 'gainst any, but in you alone
My safety lies. But what is worst of all
To bear unmoved and silently is this,

                      49

They whisper dark suspicions in your ear,
And you will grow to doubt me, and then hate.
Alb. Bah! these are brain-sick fancies. Though 'twere
        true
I'll never doubt thee, Rosamund. I trust
Myself and weigh not others' fantasies.

                                [*Exit* ALBOIN.

Ros. looking after him. Yes, limed, I think, my royal
        eagle, limed.
These massive-frowning fortresses have all
Their little posterns, easy forced, when found.
I've found the key to that hard, cruel heart,
And mean to keep it till I've need of it.
For he is proud of me—I act the queen,
Even as his heart would have it, and he dreams
I love him, and him only; and to love
Is subtlest flattery. To complete the charm,
He loves me in his fashion—beautiful
I am, and know it—do not sicken him
With too uxorious dalliance or repulse
With an estranging coldness.

                        Acted well!
Played to perfection! Yet an irksome part.
Aloft on pride's chill pinnacle I sit—
Hear far below the dash of lesser passions
Bursting against its base. No pulse of love,
Of happiness, or even desire, e'er beats
In the high, frozen solitudes of my soul.   [*Exit.*

SCENE III.—Another part of the Palace.

ROSAMUND *and* HELMICH.

Ros. Yes, Helmich, as we thought. I found him wroth;
Just caught the furtive malice on her face,
Turned back i' the opposite doorway. But she failed;
Perchance had roused his ire in my defence,
For he was almost tender, swore my foes
Were his, he'd never rued his choice of me,
He'd trust himself, not others. Though he tush'd
At my suspicions, I could plainly see
How true they were.
Hel. My queen, you may be sure
I bring no idle tales to you, nor raise
Baseless suspicions. Godeberta thinks
You stand alone, save Alma, who counts not.
I wear two liveries—yours is ever on,
The other, but a cloak to keep it safe.
When the queen-mother summons me, I don
My cloak and listen. Cautiously, at first,
She talks, not lovingly of you, but yet
Careful to veil her purpose 'and her hate.
Then, with premeditated stumble, I
Let fall some phrase unjust of you and beg
Humbly she name it not, as though in fear.
She promises; I make pretence to show
My inmost thoughts, as though I hated you.
Then falls she like ripe apple to the hand,

And all her fears, suspicions, purposes
Pours in my ear. Thereon I give advice—
Most excellent no doubt,—yet all in vain,
For aye untoward chances frustrate it.
You understand me, lady ?

Ros.   Yes, too well.
Yes, 'falls she like ripe apple to the hand,'
That is the sentence that you pass on me
To Godeberta. Think not I can trust
Such doubleness. Yet pause before you dare
My utmost vengeance. I had thought you knew
Too much to tamper with me thus, Helmich.

Hel. No need of threats or fear. I spoke amiss
To say I wore your livery; no mere livery
Is my allegiance to you. Dare I speak,
I could discover how indissoluble
The bonds that bind me to you.

Ros.   Then, speak on,
And I will try to conjure up belief
In your avowals.

Hel.   Then, the bond is love.
Yes, Helmich's love has dared to fly as high
As Alboin's.   [*Falling on his knees.*
          O my queen, fair Rosamund,
Who art the only passion of my life,
Thy beautiful, proud image is enshrined
Eternal in my heart, and all my being
Burns up in one fierce flame of passionate,
Rapt adoration.

Ros.   Helmich, rave not thus !
Dost thou forget that I am Alboin's queen,

For ever by all laws of God and man
Forbidden thee ?
        Yet, if thou would'st have hope,
Befriend your queen in her necessity.
Love long hath died in me—the word is strange,
And seems to rise from out the buried past
A spectre pale. Go, Helmich,—but remember,
Your only hope is—aid to me, at need. [*Exit* HELMICH.
He too is mine ; mine wholly.
                            [*Exit.*

SCENE IV.—*Alma's Chamber.*

ALMA *alone, sings.*

I stole my warrior to meet ;
  I love him as I love my life,
And O his words they had been sweet
    To maid or wife.

The moon was bright, the night was blue ;
  I love him as I love my life,
But O his words they were not true
    To maid or wife.

Sweet blew the winds from glades of pine ;
  I love him as I love my life,
His kisses were more warm than wine
    To maid or wife.

Before the breeze the weak grass bent;
  I love him as I love my life,
Could I from him withhold consent,
  As maid or wife?

'Alas!' I sobbed, 'I am undone;
  I love thee as I love my life,'
He kissed my frail tears one by one.
  No maid! no wife!
        [Rises and puts on cloak and veil.

Ah me! But love is very sweet;
  I love him as I love my life,
Now must I go my love to meet,
  Nor maid, nor wife.   *[Exit.*

SCENE V.—Room in Peredeo's House.

Peredeo, *pacing about restlessly.*

Wish she would come; and yet half wish it not.
Her innocence and trustfulness do make me
Remorseful. When- I talk of love to her,
I lie—yet lie not. For I love her well,
Most fondly, dearly, passionately love her:
Still not enough, and yet,—perhaps, too much.
I know not how it is. My lies would shame
A twice-bought spy, yet do I deem them truths

In speaking them.
                                Love is a demon-god ;
His feet are in hell, his head is in the heavens.
Marry her ? There Ambition doth forbid me
And, pointing to an heirless crown, doth whisper
Of politic alliance, that may strengthen
My claim and gain me suffrages, or buttress
The throne that I ascend.
                                Faith ! marry her,—
And douse poor Cupid, as these Southerns say,
In Hymen's chilly waters ? No, not I.
But now she comes.   [*Exit.*

SCENE VI.— *Banquet Hall in Palace.*

ALBOIN, ROSAMUND, GODEBERTA, CHEF, PEREDEO, ALMA,
HELMICH, MINSTREL, GUESTS, ATTENDANTS, *&c. at a Banquet.*

Alb. Curse on these times of puling peace! I say.
    Life grows disgustful, like a stagnant pool,
    One's blood goes thick and slow, one's limbs, lethargic
    Sigh as they move, weary of their own weight,
    Like over-fattened oxen. 'S death ! we rust,
    As our good blades do, i' the damp air of peace.
Ros. My liege, have not your conquests sated you
    Of slaughter ? Is't not better to behold
    Your populous cities teem with the increase

Of prosperous lands, than see the ruin's smoke
And corn down-trodden in the bloody mire?
Gode. Peace, like the unhealthy heat of southern noons
That breeds putridity, begetting swarms
Of nocuous vermin, is the hatching time
Of foul intrigues and dark, insidious plots;
. Death haunts the goblet proffered with a smile,
Leaps from the dagger plunged at dead of night.
Chef. My liege, no less achievment 'tis to knit
Together to one kingdom conquered lands,
And gather up the reins of governance
Tight in the fingers, than to win them first.
Alb. Plague on your windy wisdom! There's no good
In drowsy peace but wine. Fill, fill and drink,
Till all your blood dances with ruby fire!
Give the old minstrel drink! Warm his old
   heart!
Come, ancient, stir us with some battle strain!

Minstrel sings.

From the far north we come,
   From our stern icy home,
Home of the tempest and realm of the snow,
Where the storm rages wildly and bleak the winds blow,
   In the far, frozen realm of the snow.

To the soft, sunny south,
   Where, with grape-stainèd mouth,
Slumbered the Southern beneath the vine shade,
By luxury sated, through plenty decayed,
   In the vine's faint, luxuriant shade.

As the torrent, snow-fed
 In its dark fountain-head,
Bursts to the valley with fetterless force,
So we burst to the south irresistible course,
 With our fierce, our invincible force.

For we fought without fear,
 And our sword and our spear
Deeply of slaughter and victory drank,
And the Southern in death's darkling agony sank,
 And our sword and our spear his blood drank.

Pour ye out their red wine,
 Bounteous blood of their vine
Deep from the skull of the foe let us quaff,
Of fresh victory dream, as we revel and laugh,
 From the skull of the foe let us quaff!

Alb. Ho, Helmich! Give the minstrel gold and wine!
 Cheer his old heart and make his old blood leap
 Right youthfully! His song has stirred my blood
 To more impetuous current, as the affray
 Of some near battle doth. Where's my skull-goblet?
 (*To a page*) Ho, boy, quick, bring it! [*Exit page.*
 Wine can never taste
 So rich and warm, nor pour such full, flush joy
 Into the heart from clinking metal cups,
 As drank from worthy foeman's bleachèd skull.
Hel. to Minstrel. Here's largess from the king to cheer
 your heart,
 And wine, he sends, to make your old blood leap.

Mins. Thor set his foemen's head upon his spear !
    He is a mighty warrior ; Thor himself
    Breathed not more death around him, as he fought.
Hel. Why, you old bletherer, must you needs recall
    Such barbarous and half-forgotten customs,
    So wantonly inhuman ?   Dost not know
    His cup is of the skull of Cunimund,
    The father of the queen ?
                (*Aside*) But softly, Helmich,
    Alboin's rash folly may your wisdom be,
    And Alboin's bane may prove your remedy.
                     [*Enter page with the cup.*
Alb. Come, fill it boy !   Wet the old skull with wine,—
    The tough skull of the stoutest enemy
    I ever vanquished.   (*Drinks.*) O delicious draught !
    Come, fill again !   My Rosamund shall drink !
Ros. My lord, the clinking metal serves me best.
    I never slew a foe.   Why should I drink
    From musty skulls ?
Alb.   What, know'st thou not this pate?
    'Tis somewhat kin to thee : thou hast seen locks,
    Gray locks, growing thereon.   'S life! dost thou scorn
    Your father's head, the skull of Cunimund ?.
Ros. I—cannot—drink.   [*Thrusting away the cup.*
Alb.   Why girl, you're squeamish grown.
Ros. seizing the cup. I drink to you—(*beneath her breath*)
    —death.
Gode. aside.   How venomous she looks !
    That loose black curl seems writhing like a snake.
Hel. aside. God blast the monster ! Her face is as a stone—
    Haggard and marble-blue,—each ebon arch

Drawn down in anguish o'er the insorbed eyes
Blank with exceeding horror.   Drunken dolt!
He wounds unwittingly, like rustic clown
Crushing with heavy heel the unseen worm;
No helpless worm though, she,—can turn and bite
With fatal venom.

Chef. aside.   A rash stroke, my liege,
To bait her thus.   This queenly Rosamund
Beneath her haughty languor hath, methinks,
Some tigerish passions, dangerous to awaken.

Per. to Alm. The callous-hearted tyrant!   How the queen
Holds silence thus I know not.   I could slay
The monster as he sits.

Alm.   Peredeo,
How ghastly Rosamund looks!   I think I'll go
And ask her, if it please her to retire.

[*Curtain falls.*

SCENE VII.—*Corridor in Palace.*

PEREDEO *and* HELMICH.

Per. What, Helmich!   Such impassioned countenance
Thou seldom wear'st, and yet such cruelty
May well move indignation.   I can fight;
My foes find that,—but this grim torturing—
A woman too—I leave to fiends and Alboin.

Hel. Her friends are few; it was a dastard's part,
 Unworthy of a warrior and a king.
Per. 'Zounds! were she kin to me, he'd find my sword
 Could bite as keenly 'gainst him as for him.
 I've served him long, yet with but little love.
 He ever sets that smooth-tongued charlatan,
 Dropping his oily prudence in his ear,
 Before me—Chef, I mean, of course;—but you
 Are moved beyond your wont.
Hel.   With you I care not
 To keep my mask on.
Per.   One would think there burnt
 No passions in you, for your countenance
 Seems, water-like, to take its colour from
 Surrounding nature, unperturbed within.
 All seem to hold you in like confidence
 And Alboin, Godeberta, Rosamund,
 All dream you're theirs, and two of them are fools:
 If not all three.
Hel.   Yes; two of them are fools,
 That is, there is but one of them for whom
 My safety, pleasure or ought dear to me
 Should ever lie in real jeopardy.
 This in thine ear, Peredeo. For the queen
 I would do much.
Per.   Hers seems the losing side.
Hel. It shall not be, nor would you, an you knew her,
 So judge.
Per.   I always wondered and admired,
 Since first I saw her, with such queenly scorn,

Move mid her fellow-captives—and you know
I love my little Alma.
               But we'll talk
Our treason safer otherwhere, farewell !   [*Exit.*
Hel. looking after him. If you, hot-blooded warrior had
    been ta'en
With this mad passion, I had wondered not ;
But at myself I do ; for I had dreamt
No fire dwelt in me with the heat to thaw
The frozen armour of philosophy,
A youth neglected and unloved had left,
Sole gift, that my cold heart might rest unmoved,
As Alpine peaks beneath their sheathing snows
Eternally 'tower o'er torrent-furrowed vales.
I've heard there is a mountain where the snow
Sleepeth securely many seasons through,
Till to its unseen heart a shuddering comes,
And strange wild throes convulse it, and black smoke,
Thrust through the hollow peak, doth soil the snows;
Forth leaps the red flame and the burning streams
Hiss down the scathèd sides, impregnable
To any summer. Such a thing am I.
                 [*Paces about meditatively.*
Alas ! It is the unattainable
That lures us with completest pertinacy ;
No thrush's nest can draw a boy's desire,
As the rook's, rocking 'mid the topmost boughs.
Enough, 'tis so !—my passion has grown strong
Upon the crumbs of Hope Despair let fall.
But now, at last, I see the steep, wild path,

Slippery with treason, that may lead to her,—
That, though o'erhanging the unplumbed abyss
Of Alboin's utmost wrath, yet shall be trod.
So, like a hardy climber, I must fix
Gaze on the prize, nor ever look below.

                                        [*Exit.*

ACT IV.

SCENE I.—Balcony of Rosamund's Chamber.

Rosamund *alone.*

Ros. All fire! all fire!
 Flame in the air and burning in my heart!
 The night breeze scorches like a blast from hell,
 The stars are dancing in a maze of flame.
 O whirling brain be still, that I may form
 Curses to slack the hot fire in my heart
 And give its frantic-seething lava vent!
 Nay, I'll not curse. O fiery soul, seethe still;
 Nought ever can appease thy heat but blood!
 Cool, cool, mad brain and back thou hissing tide
 Of Passion! I must think, nor let one drop
 Of fury ebb from me, until the time.
 Blow, blow thou icy wind, thou canst not freeze
 My rigid purpose firmer than it is!
 Ye steel glittering stars again are still!
 But ye shall nevermore be stars to me,
 But dagger points, that point me to revenge.
 Thou, young pale moon, art like a sickle, that
 Shall reap for me the harvest of my vengeance!
 Ha! I can quench you all in Alboin's blood.

O cursèd, cruel, savage murderer !
If God or Satan, heaven or hell can help,
Thou shalt be slain and I will slay thee too.
Back, curses vain ! back ! ye must bide your time.
Hist ! I am mad to rave thus, frantic words
Spill no man's blood and cannot wreak revenge.
Slowly my brain seems to be swaying back
Into coherence.—Yes ; help I must have—
Haste shall not risk defeat.   The slow-hound Hate
Fleshes his fangs, when swift Rage misses hold.
No ; I can wait, the sweeter when it comes.
Helmich.   Yes, Helmich, cunning, wily, cruel,
But mine.

      Yet Helmich, cringing, subtle Helmich,
Is he the stuff that murderers are made of ?
The sword is not his weapon, dexterous words,
Intricate plots, schemes and conspiracies,
For other actors, are his proper part ;
And he shall play them and yet more for me.

And can I bear to see the monster more,
And yet not plunge a dagger in his heart ?
Yes, yes, my hatred is too deep for rage
I dared not smite him, while, I feared to fail.
My hope of vengeance is too sweet for haste.

          Enter ALMA.

Alm. How fares my Rosamund ? The cool, sweet breeze
Is so delicious after the close, hot,
And noisy air of the banquet. But how cold
And damp your hands are ! Wilt not come within.

Ros. aside. But what of her? Is't safe to trust the care
Of guilt so precious in such feeble hands?
Such load would crush this simple butterfly
With the sheer weight.
(*Aloud*)   No, I feel better here.
Alm. How cruel Albion was! how horrible
To drink from human skulls! But Rosamund,
These Lombards are so barbarous and inhuman,
And so delight in blood—the tales they tell
Of former times make one grow faint with horror
And haunt with hideous phantoms all one's sleep.
O Rosamund, Rosamund, I sometimes wish
That they had slain us.
Ros.   That I always wished.
You, Alma, pleaded peevishly for life.
Alm. I did not think life could be so unhappy,
So dark and cold, as here it is sometimes.
Ros. Say, always, Alma. Hast thou ever known,
Thou, with thy childish buoyancy of heart,
Joy, love or sympathy, since that ill hour
We thrust away the peace-fraught cup of Death?
Alm. No, not for long, long after we came here.
Ros. What mean you, Alma? Could you ever learn
To love this life?
Alm.   Not till I learnt to love.
I have deceived you, Rosamund. Forgive me!
We seem to grow estranged in this chill air.
I should have told you, for you were my friend
And elder guardian-sister, and, besides,
My mistress and my queen. I've loved too much.

In the mad stream of love I was whirled down,
Down, whither only passion reasonless
And checkless could have borne me.
        [Burying her face in her hands, and weeping.
                      O Peredeo,
Thy bluff, kind face, thy soothing, flattering voice,
Thy warrior form, without the tiger heart
These Lombards carry, has been my undoing.

Ros. Alma, I've heard thy tale, too common tale,
Of reinless, lawless love; a darker one
May yet be mine. Alma, I hate my husband';
Yes, hate him with such hatred his life's blood
Alone can quench it.

Alm.   O my Rosamund,
How terrible! I'm lost by too much love.
But deadly hatred is more terrible.

Ros. Hist girl! my life, the purpose of my life,
And your life hang upon those trembling lips.
Perhaps 'twas mad to trust you.

Alm.   No, 'twas not.
The grave keeps not the dead more dumbly safe
Than I shall keep your confidence; for I love,
Yes I do love you, though you seem so cold
And distant to me. They shall pluck this tongue
Off from its quivering roots before the secret
It holdeth.   *[A knocking is heard.*

Ros.   Alma, some one knocks within.
See who it is; if Helmich, bring him hither.
                      [Exit ALMA.
I fear I erred to tell her—she means well,

But is infirm of purpose, of resource
Too barren.

Enter ALMA and HELMICH.

Hel.   O, my queen, what wanton wrong!

Ros. Hush, Helmich ! for my hate doth need no fan.
No ; proud dislike and chilly lack of love
Were waked to fiercest hate to-night.   Speak not
O' the cause !   Go, Alma, and keep watch within.

[Exit ALMA.

I must keep calm and not unleash my rage
Till the fit moment.   Blood shall flow for blood,
Yea Alboin's lifeblood flow to slake revenge.
Now, hark ye, Helmich, now your time is come,
The prize you say you covet 'bove all prizes
Lies in your grasp, if you have bravery
Enough to win it.   Rosamund is yours—
Soul, body, all ; even the burnt-out heart
May yet rear flame of gratitude to you,
If you can dare and do.

Hel.   O Rosamund,
For such a prize it needs not courage to stake
All, now and ever ; it is simple prudence.
Pain, death, damnation are as dust o' the balance
Weighing 'gainst thee.

Ros.   No time for lovers' oaths.
Think for me—plot and act.   Can we alone
Certainly compass this ?

Hel. after a pause.   Too great a risk.
Even his unarmed violence might defeat
Our leaguèd strength.   Besides, though 'twere accom-
    plished,

We face a certain and dishonoured fate,
Unshielded by a more illustrious name
Than Helmich's; for the judgment would go thus ;
The queen had sinned with Helmich, and in fear
They slew the monarch.   Ignominious death
And brand of common caitiffs would be ours.

Ros. Whom then would'st thou entangle in our plot ?

Hel. Peredeo is my hope, a valiant chief
Of an unblemished name, that could outblaze
The cloud of such suspicion ; then, he chafes
'Gainst Alboin and complains he has not justice,
For Alboin favours Chef, Peredeo
Feels wronged and jealous.   Just to-night I met him,
Railing against the conduct of the king,
Swearing, had he had any kin to you,
It had been swift avenged, and then he doats
On Alma, and might help you for her sake.

Ros. Then sound him further, Helmich.   If 'tis well,
As yet apprize him not of our design.
Bring him to me that, being closeted
With you and me, he may already seem
To stand within the threshold of the plot.

Enter ALMA.

Alm. Quick, Helmich ! Alboin comes.

Hel.   Farewell my queen !

[*Exit* HEL.

Ros. To-night he clasps his murderess to his arms.

[*Exeunt ambo.*

SCENE II.—Room in Palace.

GODEBERTA *and* ALMA *meeting.*

Gode. How does your mistress ? On the banquet night
    She looked but ill, and suddenly forsook
    The feast. I fear that Alboin's thoughtless jest
    About the wine-cup has offended her.
Alm. It was a heartless jest.
Gode.   It is his way,
    And I myself have suffered much from it—
    None more, and yet I resolutely cast
    Such memories out of mind, for well I know
    'Tis not from hate or even lack of love,
    But from a certain callousness that grows
    Upon a warrior's heart, too much inured
    To sight of pain and death, these cruelties,
    Or what seem cruelties, do spring. Yet hard
    They are to brook, and in so proud a heart
    As Rosamund's may rankle bitterly,
    Though she keep silence. Yes, poor girl, 'twas hard,
    Still she would scorn my pity and advice.
    You will not trust me, Alma, when I say,
    I love her. Yet her loneliness and high,
    Unflinching and unswerving majesty
    Have moved a heart, once hostile, unto love
    And admiration. Think not I speak smoothly
    To wring from your fidelity betrayal
    Of confidences she reposed in you.
    I would but ask you, think you not that I

Both loving Alboin, knowing well his faults
And meaning well for her, might serve them both
Clearing the mists of coldness and dislike
That mutual failings, but ill understood,
Do breed between them?

Alm.   Yes, perhaps you˙might.
(*Aside*) I would that Rosamund had not consigned
This dreadful, fateful secret to my care.
I fear I let it slip me drop by drop.
(*Aloud*) And yet—there is no coldness or dislike,
In Rosamund at least.

Gode.   There, girl, you lie.
Dream not to hoodwink me, I know it all;
Can read her subtly governed countenance.
She loves not Alboin,—she imagines Helmich
Is with her; she is wrong.   Come, girl, confess!
You shall be safe, you may save Rosamund.
Yes, I can screen you both, if you confess.

Alm. aside. O mercy! all is out˙ if Helmich's false,
(*Beginning to weep*) O God! what shall I do? Oh
dear! Oh! Oh!

           Enter ROSAMUND.

Ros. What's this? What! Alma weeping? Now, child, go,
She shall not make me weep.   [*Exit* ALMA.
                        So, Godeberta,
You've chidden and railed at the poor girl to tears.
Pray what's the offence?

Gode.   She had no cause for tears
Save a sore conscience and a guilty heart;
And those you share, though you are dead to shame
And doubtless will outbrazen it bravely still.

Ros. Black hearts breed black suspicions, but I fail
  To catch the purport of your vehemence.
Gode. Conscience might aid you, if you let it speak.
  Down, and confess to me, before I let
  The light of day flash full upon your crime
  That lurks in darkness.
Ros.   Pray explain yourself.
  (*Aside*) She shall not worm from me aught worth
      the knowing.
  She has been sounding Alma, and I hope
  I have not come too late.
Gode.   Utterly shameless !
  And dare you gaze unflinching on the face
  Of her, whose son you hate and plot against ?
  Of course you are all innocence, of course
  You feel an indignation past the power
  Of prudence to restrain.
Ros.   No, I do not ;
  Though I am innocent, I do not feel
  The astonishment I might do, were I new
  To your intrigues against me.   I remember,
  Not long ago, I found the king much moved
  And caught your visage in malignance turned
  In the opposite doorway, and I read your work
  On Alboin ; yes, you tried to poison him
  Against me, and you failed, and still you fail.
              Enter ALBOIN.
  Alboin shall judge between us even now.
Alb. Tut, what a shrewish jar and clamour's this ?
Ros. I am his wife, and he shall hear me first.
  My liege, I came, but a few minutes since,

And found your mother, like a savage hawk
With captive pigeon, threat'ning my poor Alma.
And she, with her fierce attitude and look,
Had moved the girl to tears, and when I came
To bear her from her talons, she forsook
Her weaker prey and, facing round on me,
Poured forth vague accusations and wild threats,
As though she thought to fright me to confess
Some hidden guilt.   I, catching not the drift
Of her vain volubility, request
Particulars, and then she charges me
With hate and machinations against you.
Judge you between us.   If you credit her,
Shrink not to cast me from the eminence
You raised me to.

Gode.   But hear me now, my son !
    Not for my own life anxious or alarmed
    For my own safety, but for yours, I watch.
    I marked her, when you offered her the cup,
    The skull-cup, fashioned from her father's skull.
    I caught the glance of rage inalienable
    She shot upon you.

Alb.   'S death I'll hear no more.
    Curse on you for a pair of squabbling shrews !
    I take not Rosamund for such a fool
    As rid her of her only benefactor.
    To such a girl a living husband is
    More worth than waggon-loads of slaughtered sires.
    Now, hark ye, dame !   I told you long ago,
    'Tis at the peril of your tongue you speak
    'Gainst Rosamund to me.   Settle your strife

Between you, with your nails, an you like that.
Bring not your quarrels here, for if you do
Again appeal to me, then one shall budge,
And tough old crones are easier dispensed with
  Than young and handsome wives.   [*Exit* ALBOIN.
Gode.   Ungrateful wretch !
Ros. So, lady-mother, though the scent was strong,
  You face a barrier that will keep you long.
                            [*Exeunt ambo.*

SCENE III.—Room in Palace.

ROSAMUND *alone, pacing about.*

Ros. Just as in feverish haste the dicer's hand
  Trembles with the desire to clutch the dice,
  Upon whose final cast his all depends,
  So am I restless with strange eagerness
  To make my venture.   But I think they come.
         Enter PEREDEO *and* HELMICH.
  Welcome, my brave Peredeo ; so you come,
  With such unutterable nobleness,
  To be the champion of a woman wronged,
  Who could command no other sword but thine.
Per. Fair queen, I have, perhaps, too soft a heart,
  One that revolts 'gainst all cold cruelty,
  Surges with indignation at the thought

Of wrong upon the unoffending wrought ;
But injured beauty helpless moves me most.

Hel. Say not too soft a heart, but one attempered
By mercy, that yet slacks not bravery.
But one thing I would blame you in, my lord,
You are too patient in your own behalf,
Have suffered men in valour and in worth
Inferior far to seize the posts you claimed,
With greater merit—too much modesty,
Too much forbearance, grow in you to faults.

Ros. I well believe it, Helmich.   I have marked
(*To Per.*) The post of honour, surely due to you,
Bestowed upon another, Chef perhaps,
Who could as well withstand you, as a boy
Could bar the path of an infuriate boar.
'Tis time you struck, and boldly, for your rights.
The king has been unjust to you ; perhaps
The injustice is the fruit of jealousy.

Per. Zounds! that he has, and I have warned him often,
My patience has its limits.

Ros.   Listen, then.
Our aspirations have one common goal.
Does helpless beauty move you, beauty wronged ?
Men call me fair.   Judge you of that.   I know
That I am wronged, irrevocably wronged.
God knows, I have no champion but you ;
So I am helpless, if you help me not.
You know my tale, you can recall that day,
That sanguinary day, when Cunimund,
My father, fell, whom, with heart-rooted love
That clung about my inmost soul, I loved,

And my two brothers died in his defence.
By cruellest tyranny and direst fate
I was compelled to wed the conqueror.
I could not love him, could but keep my hate,
A fettered fiend—but it has broken loose,
His own hand burst its bonds and set it free.
I wonder such a man as you could sit
And tamely see insufferable pain
So ruthlessly inflicted.   You know well
My meaning.   On that ill-starred banquet night,
(Ill-starred for him) he proffered me the cup
Formed in the fiendish custom of your race,
Formed of a skull, and of my father's skull;
Then, first, the horrible reality
Broke on me, I had wed the very man
Whose sword was stained with my father's blood.
Since then my mind has had one only thought,
My heart has ever ached with one sole thirst,
My tongue has silently rolled one single word,
It is Revenge—it is Revenge, Revenge!
Dost understand me, sir?   Alboin must die.

Per. No, lady, no; if this be your request,
Peredeo's blade shall bear no monarch's blood.

Ros. Durst thou refuse me?   Is thy bravery
An idle vaunt? or does the name of king
Frighten you, as a child is scared with sound?
He is a monster, and unfit to live;
It is a righteous and a glorious deed
To rid the world of such.   Bethink thyself,
And be a man and, with a single sweep
Of thy good blade, revenge thyself and me.

Hel. Remember, ere you scorn your own advantage,
 And spurn a proffered crown, remember this :
 In peace your sun declines, and even now
 Is verging towards eclipse. If you strike now,
 While memory of your valour still is fresh,
 And rid a nation of a tyrant, borne
 Only through abject terror, then your hope
 Of kingdom will look brighter than it can be
 For ever after.

Per.   I am no base felon
 That, for my own advancement, murder men
 I' their beds at midnight. In the open field
 I never turned, I never held my hand,
 But slew and slew until the set of sun.
 And I confess to meet him face to face
 And blade to blade were only madness sheer.

Ros. Yours is a brutish courage, the wild rage
 Of beast of prey, and not the stern resolve
 And lofty resolution worthy man.
 - Thou art a wretched cowering thing that durst not
 Dare what thou dost desire ; this tawdry show
 Of fearless valour and great gallantry
 Yields at a touch and shows the craven core
 Of cowardice within.

Hel.   Bethink you still.
 Love you not Alma ? She is in the toils
 Of this conspiracy and, if it fail,
 She is involved in our common fate.
 You say you love her. She has yielded up
 Her heart to you, and that most dearly prized
 By woman has surrendered for your love ;

And you refuse to pluck her from the fate,
The almost certain fate, that trembles o'er her.
Per. No, not for Alma even shall Peredeo
    Become a regicide.
Ros.   Ignoble man !
    Who lured our confidence by cheap display
    Of noble sentiments, perhaps you'll buy
    As cheap promotion by betraying us ?
Per. You much mistake me. 'Tis not cowardice
    That holds me from this project, but dislike
    Of those base measures, which alone do seem
    To point way to success. I courted not
    Such confidence as this, nor ever dreamed
    Such fell disclosures would encounter me ;
    Yet, if a warrior's word or oath ye need,
    I give it that your secret shall repose
    Safely with me. Farewell, and gentler thoughts
    Be with you !   [*Exit* PEREDEO.
Ros.   Helmich, we had better part.
    I feel all stunned and dizzy from the shock
    Of foiled attempt and still determination
    Faints not but gathers force.
Hel.   Farewell, my queen !
    I think he will be staunch, and yet the game
    Goes sore against us.   [*Exeunt.*

ACT V.

SCENE I.—An Ante-Chamber in Palace.

ROSAMUND.

What hell-devisèd agony is this,
This rack of indeterminate dispute
Of warring passions in the inmost soul !—
Whether to leap down this abyss of shame,
That with its nameless horror sickens the soul
To utmost self-abhorrence, gazing on
The coveted and the heart-worshipped prize
Until its brightness robs the horrid gloom
Of its repulsive terror.   Or back-starting,
Back from the dizzying brink, let the prize go
Down into darkness, irretrievably.
It shall not.   No, it shall not; although hell
With all its flames and all its furies stood
Between me and my purpose !

What matter the means?   I reck not where the path
Leads through, so it but leads me to my goal.
And one fierce thought doth strengthen me and goad
Me ever onwards, that this foul device,
This necessary but nefarious crime,

Is wrong to him, is Alboin's infamy.
Here will I lurk, where Alma will not think
To encounter me, and, even now, she comes.

Enter ALMA, *muffled in long cloak and veil.*

Alm. starting. O Rosamund, I did not think— so late—
Ros. Lend me that cloak and veil, I've need of them.
Alm. I cannot—1 will fetch you others.
Ros.   No,
    These only will I have.
Alm.   O Rosamund,
    Others will serve your purpose, these alone
    Can serve me.
Ros.   These, these only can serve me.
                              [*Alma still hesitates.*
    Are my commands grown impotent but now?
    I tell you, girl, that, if you yield not these,
    You dash the only hope our project has.
    Life has for me one only charm, the lure
    Of vengeance.   Death is dearer than defeat.
    In my wide ruin, I would ruin you;
    So thwart me not, or rue the dread result.
Alm. giving her the cloak and veil. (Aside) What can
        she mean?   Some secret interview
    With my Peredeo?   And yet this disguise
    And the dark hour augur a strange design.
Ros. Thanks, girl; though now you know not my intent,
    Yet shall you see the fruit, triumphant fruit,
    Of this mysterious scheme.   Stay you within!
                              [*Exit* Ros.
Alm. I cannot plumb her.   Like a child that sits
    Beside a well-mouth tossing pebbles in,

79

And listening vainly for their plunge below,
So drop I my surmises in the deep
Of her dark nature, but all answerless.
Why should she need this very cloak and veil,
In which well-known disguise I pass the guards,
Upon love's errand, and unquestioned steal
Into Peredeo's chamber?   Can she mean
Revenge upon him for refusing her?
O dear I am so miserable—I wish
She would return, or I dare follow her.
Or is he false to me and does she screen
Her good name under mine?
                              I cannot wait—
At all risks I will follow.   If I find
Peredeo's false, they may discover then
That I have passions that can cope with hers.
If he is false, I reck not then what comes,
The only light in my dark life goes out.

                                   [*Exit.*

SCENE II.—*Ante-Chamber in Peredeo's House.*

Enter PEREDEO AND ROSAMUND *cloaked and veiled.*

Per. Farewell, my Alma, since the chary night
        Refuses further curtain to our love.
             [*Rosamund turns to him and lifts her veil.*
        (*Starting back*) Not Alma! O ye gods, it is the
             queen!

(*Aside*) What mazing transformation! what swift
    change !
But now my Alma's arms were round me cast,
My lips are sweet still with her kisses warm.
(*Aloud*) O my fair queen, O lovely Rosamund,
I did not think that one so high had stooped
To love Peredeo.

Ros.   You were right, my lord.
Not Love's bright fingers beckoned me to this
'Twas Hate's dark hand that dragged me on to this.
You thought to baulk me of my prey, my lord,
And by refusal have me at your mercy ;
But things are changed and you lie now at mine.

Per. How so ?   A woman's name is more to her,
Yours, lost in such bold fashion, more to you,
Than my repute for chastity can be.

Ros. My name is nought to me, my life is nought,
    Weighed 'gainst th' intense and all-absorbing passion
That rules my life.   So, if you dare to dare
The utmost vengeance of an injured man
And foully wronged husband, and the power
And pain-fed, torture-loving cruelty
Of Alboin, then refuse me my petition.

Per. O I can clear myself ; 'tis easy shown
You came not in your own but Alma's guise.
The palace-guards, and my attendants too,
Took you for Alma.   So my tale is clear
And credible, and I go innocent.

Ros. And think you that a tyrant jealousy-mad
Will trust your garbled tale of innocence ?
Will passion heed, though justice might give ear ?

Your safety bears there on a rotten branch,
That snaps at a touch.   You might as well attempt
To stay a wolf-pack with an argument,
As stay his sightless fury with such tale.
Per. aside. Curse on her, she has pushed me to a pass,
Where two paths only open their black jaws
Of Murder and Death ; so I in self-defence
Must compass murder.   'Zounds ! twere hard to die
For undesigned adultery.
            (Aloud) Yes, too true.
Ros. Then linger not with fatal hesitancy
Upon the brink of action.   Plunge at once !
            Enter ALMA.
Plague on the girl !   What fiend has led her here ?
Alm. aside. O black forebodings, ye were but too true !
(To Per.) Hands off ! for even I am much too pure
For touch of falsity so foul as thine.
Coward, deceiver, no more those lips, tainted
With broken oaths, shall press sweet poison to mine.
Fitter for Rosamund, so poison poison
Shall meet.   Go dally with your royal love !
I am a humble flower that lowly growing
Do court destruction of the reckless heel.
Tread on and fear not !   I have no great friend
To avenge my wrongs.
                    And yet, my haughty queen,
Who crouched beneath the shield of my poor name
To hide your royal guilt ; yet is there one
Who for his own sake will my vengeance wreak.
Soft-hearted Alma, Alma you despised,
May thwart your subtlest schemes.

                  O false, false queen,
Who 'neath the cold mask of your sembled pride
Did burn with love adulterous, you shall find
That I have passions that can cope with yours.
Ros. Peace, girl, nor with your ineffectual words
Burden the air. They are to me as wind
Raving against the eternal face of rock.
But listen, lest in plotting ruin to us
You rush upon your own.
                      He is not false.
I am no rival. I have stooped to this,—
This crime from which I fain would turn my
    thought,—
But to compel him by this bond of guilt
To accomplish my desire.
Per.   Alma, hear me !
Alm. I will not hear you. You, allied in guilt,
  League in deception. But for once, false man,
Your honeyed flatteries and your sweetest oaths
Shall fail of credence. To the king I go.
Ros. No ; for, if reasoning fail, and madness plunge
To its destruction, this must stop the way.
                     [Draws a dagger.
Per. coming between them. 'S death madam ! If you
    scratch that milkwhite skin,
No bond of guilt shall save you from my sword.
But, Alma, hear me. You have wronged me much
By rash suspicion and unjust reproach ;
And yet I love with no such weakling love,
As bitter words and sudden jealousy
Can crush. Would I thus court and plead with you

Before a more loved mistress?

                         I am caught
In the net of her conspiracy, and you
Draw death on me, on her, on all you loved,
If you no longer love them, round yourself
Will spread a desolation, though you escape
The blundering vengeance of this violent man.

Alm. Do you still love me then, Peredeo?

Per. You will not trust me, Alma, if I swear.

Alm. Then swear not. I will trust without an oath.
    (*Falling in his arms*) Forgive me! If you knew the
        pain intense
That seized me at the thought you loved her more,
You would forgive the madness it begot.

Per. I do.

Ros.   Is this a time for idle love-talk?
Peredeo, ere I go, I want assurance
Of your intent. Can I rely on you
To work my will on Alboin?

Per.   It must be.
It goes against me, yet you have entoiled me
In such a snare, that my life stands 'gainst his,
So he must die.

Ros,   A warrior brave and chief
Of high repute for honour and for truth,
I trust you. Alma, you must follow me,
Forget your foolish jealousy, remember
Our former friendship and renew the love,
So suddenly suspended. I meant not
To harm you, but to bar you from the path
Of common ruin.

(*To Peredeo*) Helmich shall acquaint you
When further consultation on our scheme
Finds fit occasion.   [*Exit.*
Alm. embracing Peredeo.   Now adieu, Peredeo.   [*Exit.*
Per. Plague on this unimaginable prank
   Of fortune!   Made a regicide in spite
   Of firm resolve, a blind adulterer,
   Without the honeyed pain of conscious sin.
   I am the toy of circumstance and sport
   Of women's whims.
   And yet, therein I spy my own advance,
   And fate mayhap thus bends within my grasp
   The fruit I would not climb for.
                  Yes, the crown
   May be the meed of him who dare destroy
   This cursèd tyrant, and the prudent Chef
   May find a bolder policy o'erleap
   His slow, insidious wriggling into power.   [*Exit.*

SCENE III.—*Room in Palace.*

ROSAMUND *and* ALMA.

Alm. When first your hatred you disclosed to me
   My poor thought held it not a living thing,
   Fruitful of scheme, device and consummation,
   Skilful, unscrupulous and criminal :
   But now my weak astonished soul, amazed,

Revolted, stands aghast; as one who watches,
Beneath, a friend climb perpendicular
Smooth cliffs, to height more perilous attaining
At every effort, and at last perceives
Advance impossible and is aware
The living friend who left on this adventure,
Must shortly tumble down the slippery steep
And lie a corpse before him.   O his fear
Is less than mine is, Rosamund, who dread
Thy fall to such a crime.   By our long love,   ˙
By memories of sweet childhood, by your hopes
Of heaven, and by fear of evil doom
Hereafter, I adjure you to forbear
Your deed of vengeance.   O dear Rosamund,
Sink not your noble nature to such crime,
Even for your father. .

Ros.   Hush girl, 'tis too late
To counsel me retreat,—midway I pause not ;
For I have dyed my soul in guilt so deep
That murder will not show upon the grain,
So black it is.   As dagger to my hand,
Shall I be dagger to the hand of fate,
To work her justice and my own revenge.
Touch not the surgeon's arm ; his knife might err
Most fatally.   Let be ! and veil thy sight,
Having no soul for bloody work like this !
Thou mayst betray perhaps, but canst not save.
                              [*Exit Ros.*

Alm. In vain, in vain !   Her very calmness now.
Bids me despair of moving her.   O God,
How have I watched for moment fit to speak,

Yet feel I have mischosen—having failed !
No massive gyves could make me prisoner
More surely than I am. *I may betray,*
But cannot save. And yet the guilt of this
Rises upon me hourly, as black flood
About a lonely cottage, in the night,
Laps higher slowly on the sodden walls.
That is Peredeo's step. O would to God
I could dissuade him !   [*Exit.*

SCENE IV.—*In front of Palace Gates.*

CAPTAIN *and* SOLDIERS *on guard.*

Enter HELMICH.

Hel. Captain, I bear the queen's commands to you.
The king, o'ercome by toils and cares of state,
Already seeks his chamber for repose
So needful. To secure him undisturbed,
Unbroken rest, she bids you close these doors
And, since no more these portals claim your care,
Go forth, and glad your loyal hearts with wine !
                                [*Gives them money.*
Solds. Long may they live !
Cap.   Hist fools ! Best keep your breath
For shouting o'er the wine-cups. These commands
Shall straightway find obedience. Bolt these doors
And pass out at the postern.

Hel.   See none lounge
   About the palace, trolling drunken catches.
(*The soldiers having closed the doors pass out at the postern,*
         and Helmich shuts it after them).
1st Sol. O'ercome by toils and cares, more like by wine.
2d. Sol. He drinks in peace more than he shed in war.
3d. Sol. He was a glorious fighter, lopped his foes,
   As one lops poppy-heads off with a switch.
4th. Sol. But he was very bloody, never seemed
   Sated with carnage.
5th Sol.   I misdoubt me sore
   About the stealthy closing of these gates.
1st Sol. I thought it strange that he should sleep so light,
   After his drinking too, that our low chat
   Or tread of chance foot could disturb his rest.
3d Sol. In war he was no sluggard and at dawn,
   First of the host he woke, athirst for fight.
2d. Sol. 'Tis no affair of ours, we but obey.
   I never grumble while my largess lasts.
   I never break a bottle, till its empty.
           Sings.
     With enough for myself
       And a sip for my lass,
    I care not for ought,
       As I fill my glass.
Cap. entering from within.   Silence, you roystering
   knaves, and follow me!
   Remember, if the sound of drunken noise
   Pierce the hushed palace at any hour to-night,
   'Tis like the offenders shall shout little more.
                  [*Exeunt.*

SCENE V.—*Alma's Chamber.*

ALMA *alone.*

A double fear is on me, knowing now
My shame as woman must be manifest
Ere long, unless I add a crime to folly.
O me, to be a child again and sleep
To my dear mother's singing! For all sleep,—
(Sweet, peaceful arbour where the weary heart
Seeks refuge from its pain) is now denied me.
By night I hear, or fancy, stealthy steps
Pass and repass my chamber, and faint whispers,
And sudden jars that through the corridors
Give echo tomb-like; oft I hold my breath
Expectant of some sudden, violent shout
Of murdered man or shriek of woman's terror.
This (*taking up a phial*), said the doctor, would obtain
    me sleep,
And give me full forgetfulness till morn,
'This much,' he said. 'The half a dangerous,
The whole a fatal dose.' What means this fatal,—
But that I wake not when the morning comes,
Nor at the noon, nor when the sun is setting,
Nor ever any more? The whole for me!
Men tell us there is fiery punishment
Hereafter for the wicked. Am I wicked?
I would go hence to shun more wickedness.
(*Pours out contents of phial into cup*) What a mere
    driblet this to hold great Death,—

In that half mouthful.   I cannot believe it.
Some will I drink—   [*Takes up the cup.*
              And then will go to rest.
     [*She puts it to her lips.   A sudden noise is heard.*
O God, they murder him !   [*Drinks off the poison.*
              So must I expiate
My former weakness.   [*Noise ceases.*
              'Tis a false alarm.
Shall I be lost for this ?   O mercy ! mercy !
              [*Covers her face with her hands.*

O would that I could sleep me back again
To child-like innocence !   Perhaps Death wakes us,
Like some fond mother, with a kiss, forgiving
Past error, smiling off all memories dark.
I'll get me now to rest.   [*Lies down in the bed.*
                    [*Curtain falls.*

SCENE VI.—Ante-Chamber leading to Alboin's Bedroom.

ROSAMUND *and* HELMICH.

Ros. He sleeps the stupid slumber wine doth work :
   His sword hilt have I bound firm to the sheath—
   No human hand could draw it.
Hel.   All goes well ;
   The gates are fast ; the captain I can trust

To keep his men at useless distance hence.
O fairest queen, sweet prize for which I sin,
If sin it be to follow where love leads,
Art thou not nearly mine?

Ros.   No, not till he
Is dead and my hot hate is all poured out,
Can love thoughts move me.

Hel.   It shall not be long,
Peredeo's time draws near.

Ros.   I will resume
My hate-supported vigil. You watch here.
If any but Peredeo come this way,
Spare you no means to lead them from this place.
                                                            [*Exit.*

Hel. But few, so late, dare make for Alboin's room,
But one there is might greatly mar our plan,
Old Godeberta. God forbid her coming!
In the half-gloom how freely work my fears!
The heavy shadow of that curtain holds
A crouching traitor. Though I know 'tis folly,
I needs must thrust my foot there to make sure.
I listen with a timid fascination
To Alboin's labouring breath, and unshaped fear
And inarticulate dread do breathe on me
A chilly tremor. That's a step, I'm sure,
And not Peredeo's.

                    Enter GODEBERTA.

                    (*Aside*) Then, are we lost?

(*To Godeberta*) Hush! the king sleeps and Rosamund
      is within.
I would not have her know I watch without.

She bade me go,—that, since the doors were shut,
No guard was needed. Feigning acquiescence,
I went, but stole back here to make all sure.

Gode. What means the early closing of these gates
And silently-worked dismissal of the guard?

Hel. If you will come without, nor risk the loss
Of our precautions, you shall understand. [*Exeunt.*

Enter PEREDEO.

Per. Helmich not here? How strange, and past the hour!
It fits not lurking here, I should be found.
I would it were all over. Stabs i' the dark
Are not the coins I am wont to pay
My debts with.

Enter HELMICH.

Why not at your post before?

Hel. No fault of mine, for Godeberta came
Prying around here, so I must needs tice her
On some wrong scent.

Ros. opening the door and beckoning. Come, if you are
prepared.

(*They grasp their spears and go in. Rosamund shuts the
door. Sounds of struggling within.*)

Alb. within. Blast thee, false blade! art thou turned
traitor too?
But any weapon does for coward churls.

[*A heavy fall is heard.*

Ros. within. Now monster thus my father is avenged.
I warm my-dagger in that heart made hot
By hellish cruelty.

Per. within.   He can hear no more.
Upbraid not his dumb corse.

Hel. within.   Now, Rosamund,
  I claim my guerdon.
Ros. within. Leave me awhile to feast on this good sight,
  That murderous hand all nerveless and the tongue,
  That wrought a keener anguish than the hand,
  Silent for ever. 'Tis a goodly deed.
                         Re-enter PER *and* HEL.
Per. Go, Helmich, now and call our followers,
  Ere aid from any quarter can arrive.   [*Exeunt.*

SCENE VII.—Curtain rises again, showing Inner Room.

Alboin lying dead with a stool clutched in his hand.

ROSAMUND.

Ros. looking at the body. And art thou dead?
  Whom I have feared, and hated, and despised.
  And yet, through all, have felt a fitter mate,
  Worthier my love or hatred than are these
  Now living.
            'Twas untoward Fate that blew
  The battle blast between us; so, half sad
  Amid success am I, that our stern game
  Is over for ever; and, as when the fire
  That preys by night on fane or palace, streaming
  With red locks up the darkness, sinks at last
  The victim of its victory, leaving but

Black walls and heaps incinerate, so my soul
Is desolated by its own success.

. The wife of Helmich with no love for him !
Peredeo's ally with contempt for him !
Why talk I thus ?   Thou art avenged, my father,
And now more proudly in the halls of death
Thou movest 'mid the throngs of warrior souls !

And yet, O how unworthy am I now,—
Of him, the noble, honourable, true.
Away cursed doubts ! my father is avenged.
      Enter PEREDEO *bearing the inanimate body of* ALMA.
Per. This also is our work.
Ros.   How so ?—not dead ?
Per. By accident, or with desperate intent,
    She drank a fatal potion from this phial. [*Holding it up.*
Ros. Deadly recoil of our achieved success !
    (*Taking Alma's hand*) O Alma, I had given my life
        for thee,—
    Would give it now.   Cold ! cold ! Does she not
        breathe ?
Per. How have we wronged thee, pure confiding soul,
    Too tender and too guileless by the foul
    Vicinity of crime ! One cold, last kiss !
              [*He kisses her, and bows over her sobbing.*
                  Enter HELMICH *hurriedly.*
Hel. without noticing Alma, to Ros. One seal of love,
        sweet bribe, my bride to be.
Ros. turning from him. Look there !
Hel. starting back. (Aside) Ill-omened nuptials ours

Ros. speaking as though by herself. No, not until my
      purpose was accomplished.
Not e'en thy death, mine only friend, can move me
Unto repentance, neither can regret
Stab through the armour that mine ancient love
Hath mailed me in.
              And though 'twere meet to die,
I may not, being debtor unto Fate,
Self-sold to my accomplice.
                  Bring me wine!
This night is sacred to my father's spirit.
We'll shame the morn with revel, drive dull Murder
With laughter from our halls.
                    [Curtain falls.

Milton Keynes UK
Ingram Content Group UK Ltd.
UKHW010638270324
440147UK00003B/92